I0545562

TimAI

First published in 2023.
Copyright ©TimAI

All rights reserved. No part of this book may be reproduced or used in any manner without the prior written permission of the copyright owner, except for the use of brief quotations in a book review.

To request permissions, contact the publisher at
timal.publishing@gmail.com

This book belongs to

_____

At the very foot of the scary Black Mountain, which could neither be
bypassed nor climbed over, there was an immense golden field of wheat. It was so big that even the birds flying above it could not see the edge. During the day spikelets of wheat basked in the sun, and at night they either slept or argued with each other: whose number is greater - them in the field or stars in the sky?

But since it was impossible to prove who was right, after long and noisy disputes things more often than not ended up in a real fight.

Spikelets lived in families: mother, father and a bunch of children. It seems that they should all be the same, but that was very much not the case. In fact, each spikelet was special: one loved the sun and reached out for it, and therefore was long and thin, while the other, on the contrary, hid in the shade of others, seeking a cool breeze, which is why it was small and chubby.

One was tanned, the other was pale, there
were cheerful and sad ones, cheeky and shy ones,
the screamers and the quiet ones, the talkers and
those who preferred to stay silent. In short, they were
very different.

Once upon a time there lived in this field the most ordinary family of spikelets, that was not particularly different from the rest. Just like the others, they lived in their small group, always standing in one place.

They did the most ordinary things that spikelets do in life: they chatted
and gossiped a lot, from time to time they admired the
humans who appeared in the field, they were terribly
afraid of scary black crows with fiery red eyes but had
great respect for the scarecrow on a wooden stick, which
the crows regarded with great apprehension.

For the spikelets humans were super-beings on whom everything depended: how long they would live in their native field and when they would leave it. They felt that they were very important for humans, as they treated the spikelets with great care and love.

Sometimes humans carefully stepped between the straws and examined the spikelets closely, and the luckiest got strokes on the golden heads, consisting of many grains of the colour of the sun.

"Dad, I have another question!" – spikelet-son impatiently pressed his father. This little spikelet was the most restless and inquisitive of the whole family and was nicknamed Little-know-it-all.

"Of course, little one! Remind me what number is this question?" father smiled gently, "What else would you like to know?"

"But Dad! You yourself said that the more we know, the more interesting our life is! And most importantly, then we are interesting to ourselves."

"That is true" father answered thoughtfully.

"Why are we standing in one place? Why can't we walk like humans or fly like birds? What is beyond the Black Mountain? Why in one place? And what about the mountain? Why? Why? Why?" Little-know-it-all repeated, turning to look at his mum.

He was the only one from the whole family who was interested in everything at once. His brothers and sisters were not curious, they were content with the way they lived: they did not dream of anything and did
not aspire to anything, and they considered their brother not quite normal. But they also believed the ancient legend, which said that they would live a carefree life, at the end of which they would bring a great benefit to humans.

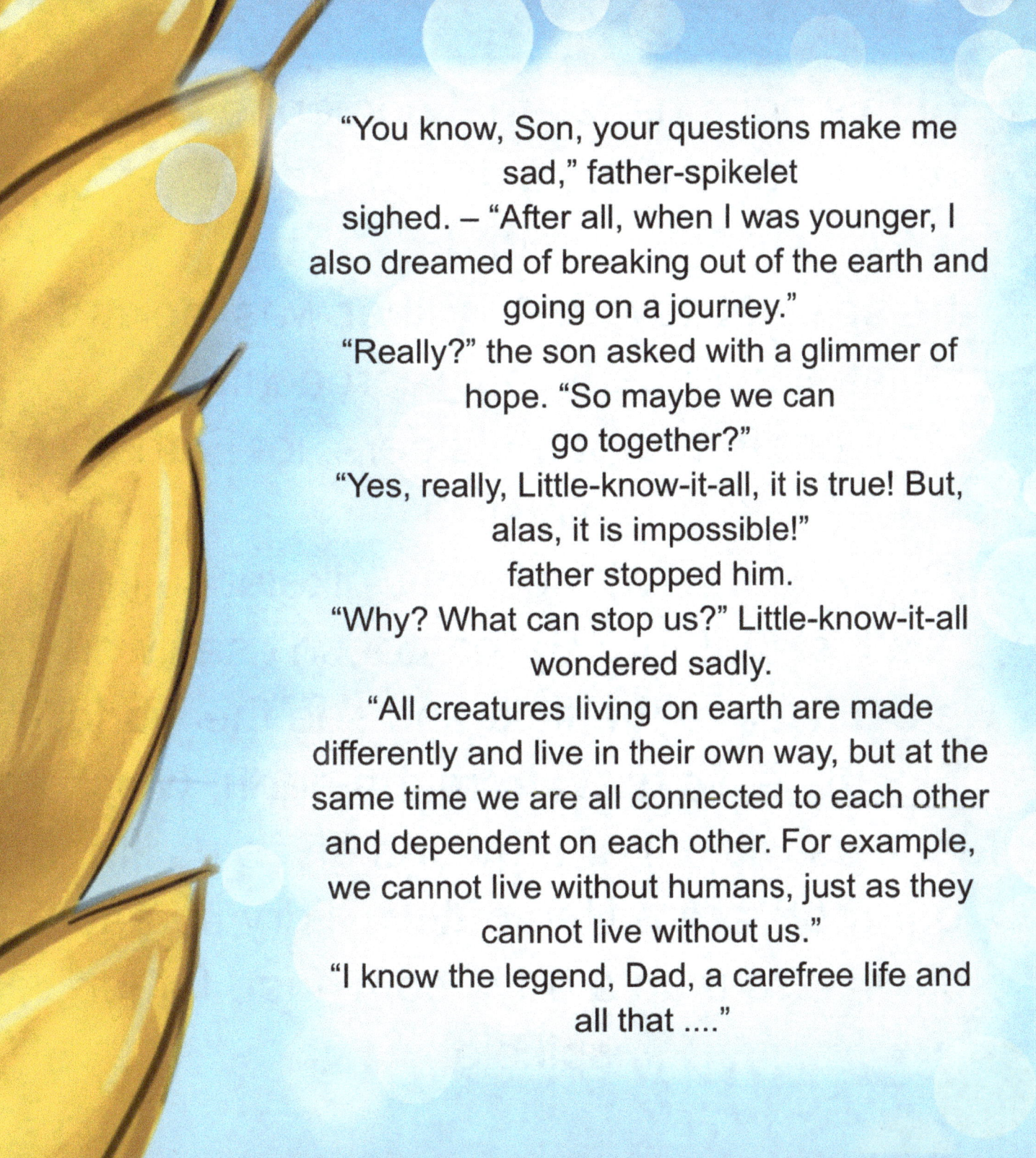

"You know, Son, your questions make me sad," father-spikelet
sighed. – "After all, when I was younger, I also dreamed of breaking out of the earth and going on a journey."

"Really?" the son asked with a glimmer of hope. "So maybe we can
go together?"

"Yes, really, Little-know-it-all, it is true! But, alas, it is impossible!"
father stopped him.

"Why? What can stop us?" Little-know-it-all wondered sadly.

"All creatures living on earth are made differently and live in their own way, but at the same time we are all connected to each other and dependent on each other. For example, we cannot live without humans, just as they cannot live without us."

"I know the legend, Dad, a carefree life and all that ...."

At this point he felt that someone poked him in the side. Turning around, the spikelet saw that mother was looking at him tenderly, but reproachfully.

"Do not interrupt the elders, let Father finish."

"Sorry, Mum," whispered Spikelet guiltily, "it's just that the legend doesn't say why we can't leave the field and see the world."

"Because we grow from the earth, which feeds us with its energy and gives us life. If our roots are pulled out we'll dry up and die in less than a day," continued father-spikelet.

"So, I will have to spend my entire life here and remain an ordinary, meaningless spikelet? So I'm not destined to become a traveller about whom legends will be told? Am I just a worthless spikelet that will soon be forgotten?! After all, we live such a short time! Is this true, Dad?" Little-know-it-all asked with tears in his eyes.

"Don't talk like that, Son! Yes, we live a short time! Yes, alone we are useless! But know that we are much more valuable than you can imagine. Our life is short, but very important. We, small spikelets, gathered together, give life to humans. And they protect us and let us live our whole lives with our families, and only when we ripen, they gather us and turn us into flour that feeds their lives," father-spikelet proudly finished.

"Yes, humans are good, unlike crows," Little-know-it-all shivered.

There were terrible rumours all over the field about black crows, both adult spikelets and children were scared to death of them.

After all, ruthless crows dug their huge claws into the unfortunate spikelets, pulled them out of the ground along with their roots and carried them away to the scary Black Mountain, where they devoured them greedily.
After talking with his father Little-know-it-all cheered up a little. The child believed him before, and believed him now, and no longer considered his life useless.

However, dreams of travel and great deeds did not disappear, they lingered in his mind.
More than anything in the world the little spikelet wanted to break away and see the world, because apart from the sky, humans, terrible crows and countless number of spikelets like himself, he did not have a chance to see anything else.

And he was sure that there are many, many more amazing and interesting things in the world.
"Eh, if I could walk like humans, or fly like birds, I would see the world, and when I returned, I would tell the whole field where I was and what I saw. My Father would be so proud of me," the child became deep in thought with slight frustration.

Life in the wheat field went on as usual; the sun brought joy with its warmth, only occasionally hiding behind the clouds, slowly floating over the field with an air of importance. Spikelets loved to watch the sky and look out for the clouds that looked like them. It happened very rarely, but when it did happen, all in the field were indescribably thrilled. The little spikelet rejoiced along with everyone, but not the same as before. After the conversation with father, he kept thinking about how to carefully, and most importantly, without being noticed by anyone, to pull at least one root out of the ground and see what would happen.

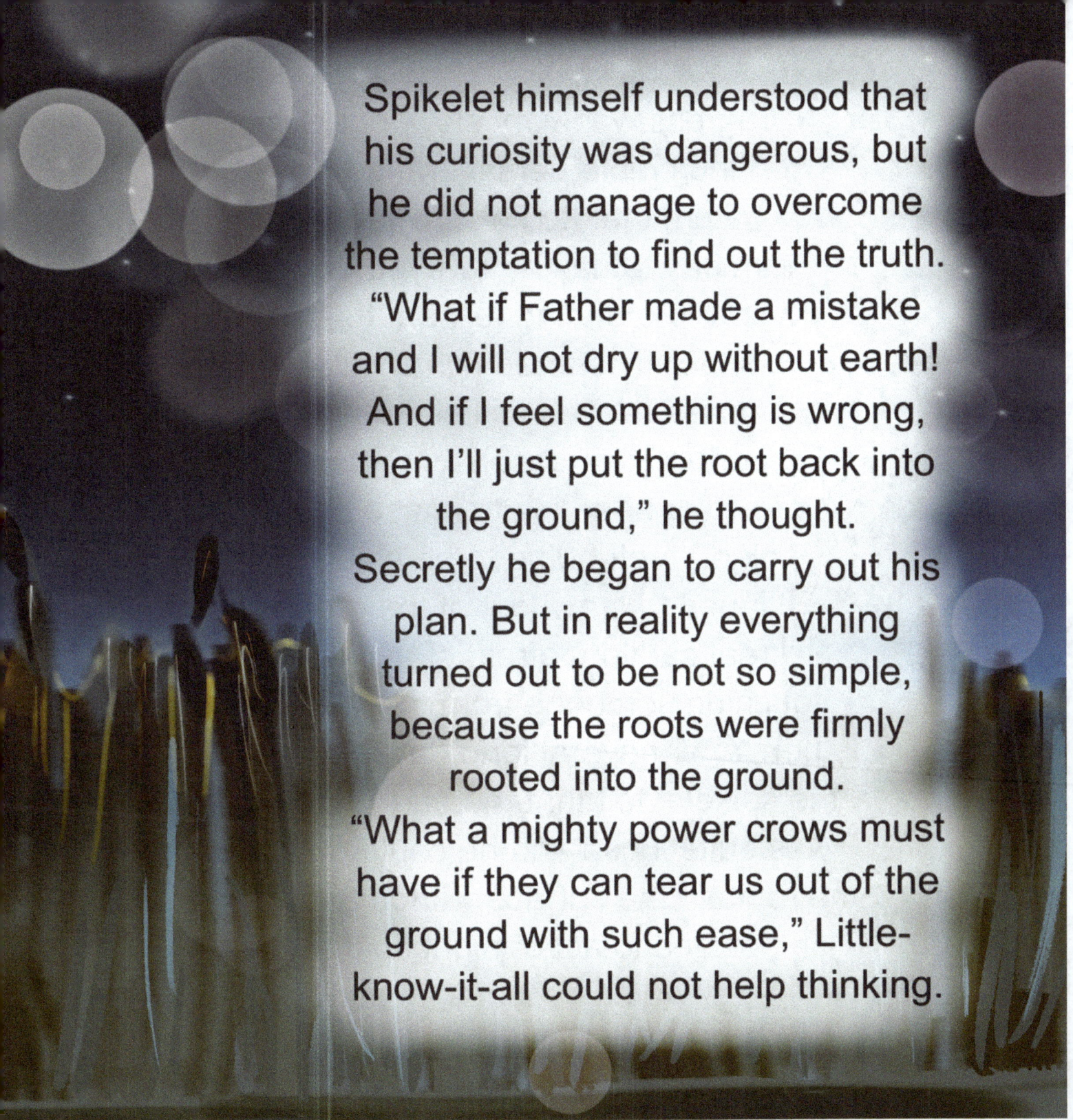

Spikelet himself understood that his curiosity was dangerous, but he did not manage to overcome the temptation to find out the truth. "What if Father made a mistake and I will not dry up without earth! And if I feel something is wrong, then I'll just put the root back into the ground," he thought.

Secretly he began to carry out his plan. But in reality everything turned out to be not so simple, because the roots were firmly rooted into the ground.

"What a mighty power crows must have if they can tear us out of the ground with such ease," Little-know-it-all could not help thinking.

Progress was very slow, but he had incredible perseverance and was determined to finish what he started. From day to day he swayed, stretched upward, pretending to want to touch the sun, specially started fights with brothers and sisters. The spikelet used every opportunity to loosen its roots without attracting attention to himself. Even at night, pretending to be asleep, he continued to crawl out of the ground with great caution, afraid of accidentally touching someone from the family. And then, after several long days and nights, the spikelet felt that the earth around him was quite loose and he could pull any of the roots to the surface without much effort. He decided to act at night so that no one would notice anything.

"Why are you so thoughtful today?" mother asked Little-know-it-all, who was gently swaying on his stem. "I was just dreaming a little! As if I'm a cloud, flying here above you, making all sorts of faces, and you don't even know that it's me. And it would be even better if I was a rain cloud, then I would pour rain on the most unkind ones, and this would make them even angrier," answered the child.

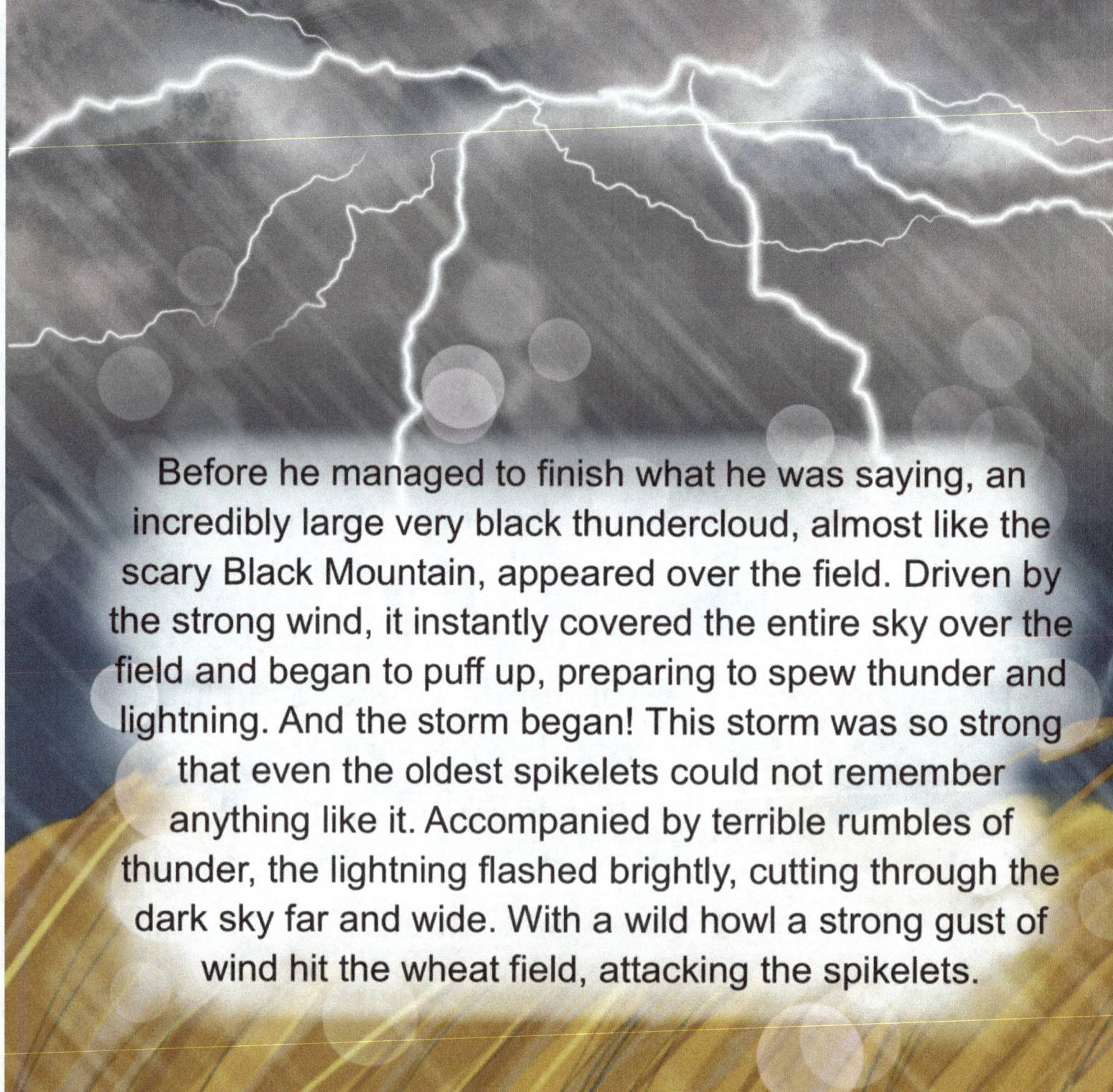

Before he managed to finish what he was saying, an incredibly large very black thundercloud, almost like the scary Black Mountain, appeared over the field. Driven by the strong wind, it instantly covered the entire sky over the field and began to puff up, preparing to spew thunder and lightning. And the storm began! This storm was so strong that even the oldest spikelets could not remember anything like it. Accompanied by terrible rumbles of thunder, the lightning flashed brightly, cutting through the dark sky far and wide. With a wild howl a strong gust of wind hit the wheat field, attacking the spikelets.

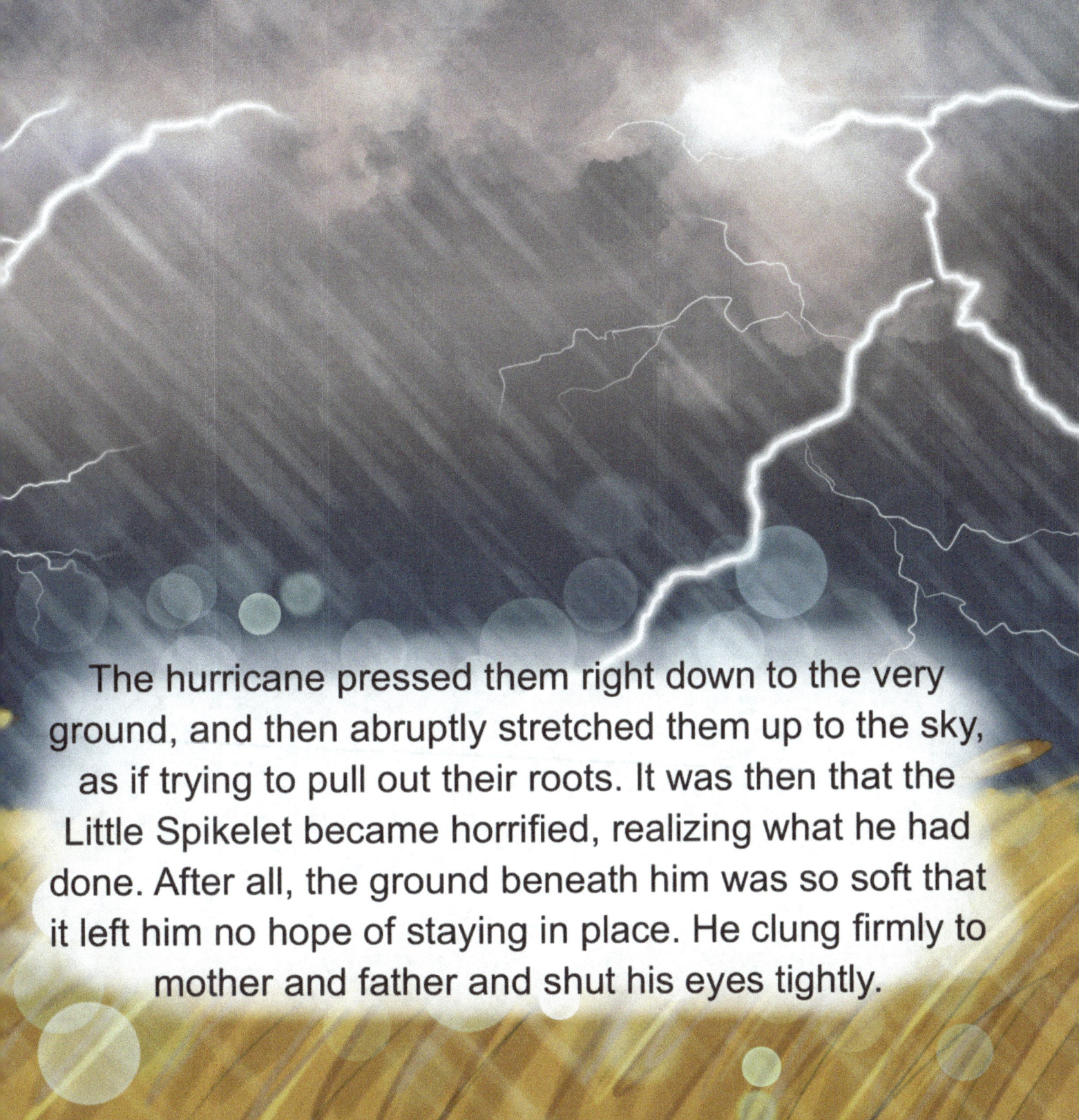

The hurricane pressed them right down to the very ground, and then abruptly stretched them up to the sky, as if trying to pull out their roots. It was then that the Little Spikelet became horrified, realizing what he had done. After all, the ground beneath him was so soft that it left him no hope of staying in place. He clung firmly to mother and father and shut his eyes tightly.

"Don't be afraid, Son, we will manage, the main thing is to stick together," father spikelet tried his best to look brave, although he was also very scared. After all, fear for your loved ones is the biggest fear of all. In the next moment, a new gust of wind flew right at their family and pulled Little-know-it-all out of the ground. Seeing what happened, the whole family grabbed the Child, trying to hold on to him, but the forces were unequal. Howling like a wild animal, the wind snatched him away and carried him high into the sky.

"Sorry, Dad," was the last thing the Child managed to shout out, flying further away and higher up from his native field. Terrified, he could not open his eyes and did not see that, carried away by the wind, he was flying straight to the scary Black Mountain.

Suddenly, the flight that seemed endless was cut short. The wind crashed into the rock, flew up and did not return. Exhausted by the hurricane and wet from the rain, Little-know-it-all slowly slid down the rock until he was on a ledge. Feeling a hard surface beneath him, lying on his side, nailed down by heavy rain, he finally dared to open his eyes.

In the rock opposite the spikelet saw a dark cave and crawled towards it with the last of his strength. And then he noticed that many fiery red eyes were slowly moving towards him from the very depths of the cave. Realizing where he was the Little Spikelet did not scream, but simply fell unconscious and lay like that all night.

When the Child woke up the storm had long passed and the sun was already high in the sky. Looking around, he realised that it was not a nightmare: Little-know-it-all saw a huge black Crow in front of him.

A few more birds sat a little further behind him, from time to time they ran their claws over the rock, making a sound that made the heart clench. Having prepared for the worst, Spikelet did not take his eyes off the crow.

"I have lived a long life and have seen many things, but never anything like this," said the old Crow, slightly tilting his head to one side, looking at the Spikelet with great interest.

"I understand that the hurricane brought you here, but still I am very surprised at how high up you ended up. It will take you a long time to get home," – croaking loudly the Crow laughed, and the rest of the crows laughed after him.

"Why all this talk, we both know what is going to happen now! Hurry up and do your dirty work" blurted out the Child, having plucked up the courage.

"What kind of work?" "Eat me alive, but hurry and be done with it," Little-know it-all hissed.

"I have lived a long life and have heard many things, but never anything like this," the Crow was again surprised.

"And I have heard everything about you and know everything about you," the Child said angrily and gasping with agitation quickly told the crows everything that he had heard about them from early childhood. The crows listened attentively and frowned heavily.

"Looking out for the weakest?" the old Crow repeated the words of Little-know-it-all. "Not at all, my little friend," – the Crow said with a soft smile and looked at the Child not with evil, cold eyes, but with the most kind eyes, like his mother and father's.

At that very moment fear left Little-know-it-all and in his heart he felt warm and calm. He could not know for sure, he just felt like he was not in danger anymore. The child was sure that someone, whose eyes look like his parents' eyes, is simply not capable of evil.

"We fly over the field not to take the weakest and most defenceless," the Crow continued.

"We want to pick up only the fallen grains and feed them to our children! Have any of you seen how we tear out a whole stalk from the ground and carry it away, devouring it on the go? I don't think so! All this is the product of your imagination, and is born from gossip and idleness," the Crow laughed.

"But what about your eyes?" Little-know-it-all asked without fear, but still timidly.

He even shivered, remembering the wild horror induced by the crows that fly over the field and look out for prey.

"They're not the same as they are now," he added, looking away. "Ah, eyes! - Those terrible, red eyes," the Crow laughed again. "We fly over the field and search for grains for a long time and sometimes in vain. Believe me, Child, it is not so easy to see the fallen grains in the field. We squint to look more closely, which is why we look angry. Now try to find the smallest pebble on the rock and you yourself will understand everything."

The spikelet immediately began to inspect the ground, scanning thousands of grains of sand and trying to find the smallest one. His eyes involuntarily began to narrow, taking on a menacing look. Although he was a young boy, he had an uncommonly vivid imagination. Imagining how he looks now, he began to smile. "Well, I see you understand what I mean," said the Crow, also smiling. "Yes, you are scarier than the scariest Crow, just frightfully scary! Now I know who to scare my children with when they misbehave!"

And they laughed together.

"And the redness of the eyes ... it's just from tiredness, sighing the Crow finished. "Forgive me," Little-know-it-all said guiltily, "it turns out that we had no reason to be afraid of you all this time?" He turned his gaze from one crow to another. "It seems this way!" the birds nodded their heads.

"We are how you see us now, not the cruel wheat-eaters from your stories. What you hear about the others does not always turn out to be true. I hope you will tell this to your relatives when I return you to the field?" said the old Crow. "Will you return me home?" Little-know-it-all asked with hope and surprise. "Of course, Child! And the sooner the better, because without earth you will die".

"Here, Father said the same thing, but I did not listen to him and almost died". The child began to tell his story, although no one asked him. The sullen crows listened attentively, marvelling at the courage and quick thinking of this inhabitant of the wheat field.

"As you can see, if you really want something, even the wildest dreams come true. But next time be careful what you wish for," the Crow said profoundly, looking seriously at his new friend.

"But it is true," Little-know-it-all carried on, - "I always dreamed of traveling and incredible adventures, and here I am, even though it almost cost me my life."

Then the squeak of chicks came from the cave: the little crows used all their strength to let their parents know that they were hungry and it was time to feed them.

"Well, my friend, it's time to fly to the field to find food for the little ones, although we may again frighten your fellows terribly," – the Crow said, with a quizzical look.

"That'll be next time!" Little-know-it-allexclaimed cheerfully. He shook his head with all his strength and golden grains fell out like drops of rain, merrily tapping on the black rock.

Seeing this, the chicks, jumping over each other, started pecking at the lunch that suddenly appeared. "Thank you!" the Crow bowed politely to the Child. Surrounded by small crows that rubbed against him in gratitude with their still unfledged bodies, he enjoyed the fact that he was able to feed the little ones and be useful to these, as it turned out, wise and kind birds.

"It is time" croaked the old Crow. He carefully took Little-know-it-all with his claws by the straw and began to rise into the sky. "Goodbye my friends!" Little-know-it-all shouted. "Goodbye!" the chicks squeaked after him. Taking off into the sky the Crow flew towards the wheat field. "Wait," said the Child, "before we go home, I will have one last request for you."

"Go on" the Crow croaked.

"Could you fly even higher so that I can at least see with
one eye what is on the other side of the scary Black
Mountain? We have always wanted to find out. And if I
am the first to find out what's out there I will return home
a real hero," the Child said dreamily. "As you say," the old
Crow answered and quickly soared high into the sky.

He slowly flapped his wings, keeping himself in the air above the very top of the mountain. On the one side the Spikelet saw his native field, whose inhabitants cheerfully met humans walking on it, and on the other, to his surprise, he saw bare land with barely any bushes growing on it. Humans also walked on the bare land, only their faces did not radiate any joy. The child could only see deep sorrow in their unhappy eyes.

"What is wrong with them?" he asked the Crow.

"They are sad that they do not have wheat, they spend their whole lives half starving and very often they cannot feed their children," answered the Crow.

The Crow held Little-know-it-all in high over the Black Mountain patiently and for a long time, while Little-know-it-all looked down silently and thoughtfully.

"Once Father told me that we are worthless alone, and that all together we are a huge force that is able to provide humans with bread. I want to be the beginning of this great force. Take me to them, my friend," the Child suddenly declared confidently.

"What about your family?" asked the wise Crow, feeling a lump come to his throat. Are you ready to sacrifice your life with your family for the sake of humans?" "All my life I dreamed of doing something worthwhile, but Father said that one cannot do it alone, I am ready to prove that this is not so. Even the smallest and weakest can become great if he devotes his life to this." "I have never seen anything like this, I have never met anyone like this. I am very proud that I have met you, my little friend," the Crow said quietly and began to descend to the bare land on the other side of the Black Mountain. Having landed, he very carefully laid the withering spikelet on the ground and immediately began to furiously dig a hole in the ground to lower the roots of the little hero into it, then he sprinkled them with earth and, without saying anything, quickly took off and disappeared into the sky. The Spikelet, standing in the dry earth, felt how the last strength was leaving him: he was drying up.

"Crow, dear Crow, you're back!" he shouted joyfully, seeing the approaching bird, and then another and another. Flying close to Little-know-it-all the birds opened their beaks, from which water flowed directly onto the ground where the Child stood. The roots, feeling the moisture, immediately began to fill with life. The Spikelet instantly got stronger and rose above the ground, confidently holding on to the stalk. The crows jumped around, loosening the earth and digging holes with their sharp claws.

"Ready?" the Crow asked, nodding to Little-know-it-all.

"Ready!" he answered firmly.

"Well! Then start your great work," croaked the Crow.

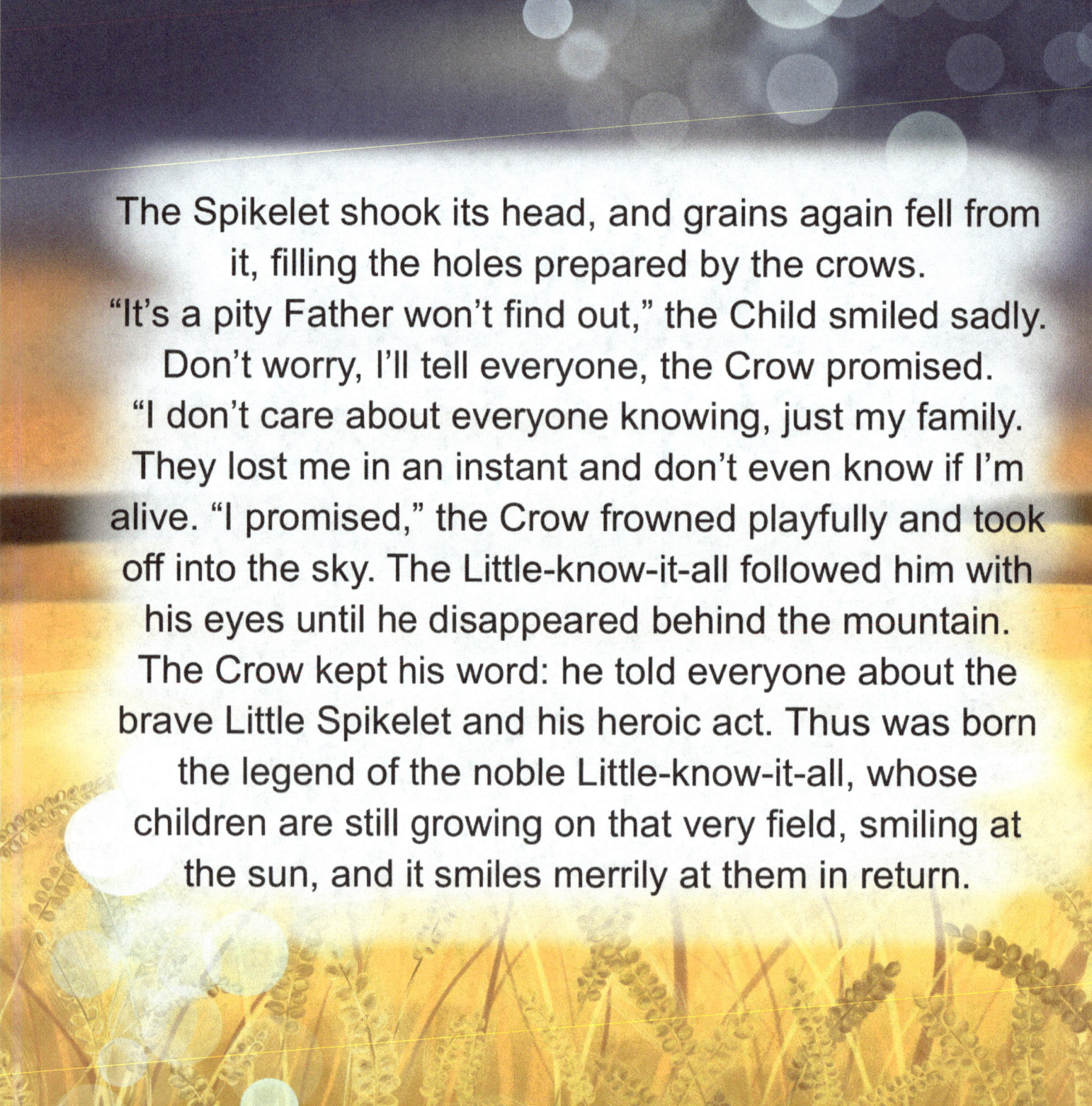

The Spikelet shook its head, and grains again fell from it, filling the holes prepared by the crows.

"It's a pity Father won't find out," the Child smiled sadly.

Don't worry, I'll tell everyone, the Crow promised.

"I don't care about everyone knowing, just my family. They lost me in an instant and don't even know if I'm alive. "I promised," the Crow frowned playfully and took off into the sky. The Little-know-it-all followed him with his eyes until he disappeared behind the mountain.

The Crow kept his word: he told everyone about the brave Little Spikelet and his heroic act. Thus was born the legend of the noble Little-know-it-all, whose children are still growing on that very field, smiling at the sun, and it smiles merrily at them in return.

What was your parents
favourite moment
during the story?

_____

_____

_____

_____

_____

_____

What was your favourite moment during the story?

_____

_____

_____

_____

_____

_____

_____

Who was your favourite
character and why?

_____

_____

_____

_____

_____

_____

www.ingramcontent.com/pod-product-compliance
Lightning Source LLC
Chambersburg PA
CBHW082017170626
46817CB00009B/3123